Small Blue

and the

DEEP

DARK

NIGHT

Jon Davis

Houghton Mifflin Harcourt
Boston   New York

www.hmhco.com

The illustrations were painted digitally.
The text type was set in Aged Book.
The display type was set in Sketch Block.

Library of Congress Cataloging-in-Publication Data
Davis, Jon, author, illustrator.
Small Blue and the deep dark night / Jon Davis.
pages cm

Summary: Small Blue is afraid that all sorts of frightening things are lurking in the dark, but as Big Brown
takes her through a dark house to warm some milk, he suggests preposterous alternatives.

ISBN 978-0-544-16466-6
[1. Fear of the dark—Fiction. 2. Humorous stories.] I. Title.
PZ7.D2933Sm 2014   [E]—dc23   2013020191

Manufactured in China
SCP 10 9 8 7 6 5 4 3 2 1
4500469151

For Laura and Greta

In the deepest, darkest hour of the night,

Small Blue woke up.

Small Blue thought of creepy things.

She thought of sneaky things.

She thought of gnarly snarly teeth,

boggling goggling eyes,

and a sniffling snuffling nose.

"Big Brown, Big Brown!" she cried.

Big Brown opened the door.

"What's the matter, Small Blue?" he asked.

"I saw goblins," Small Blue said.

"You saw goblins?" Big Brown asked.

"I didn't exactly see them, but I'm sure
they were there," said Small Blue.
"Gremlins and goblins, with empty, rumbling bellies,
licking their lips, waiting for me in the dark!"

"But if it was dark, how do you know it wasn't a delightful doggies' Saturday-night unicycle convention?" Big Brown asked.

"That doesn't sound very likely," said Small Blue.

"But isn't it just as likely as gremlins and goblins?" he asked.

"No way!" said Small Blue.

Big Brown turned on the light.

There were no gremlins or goblins.

There were no delightful doggies, either.

"Let's go have a cup of warm milk," Big Brown said.

Small Blue and Big Brown stepped into the hall.

"I can't see anything!" yelped Small Blue.

"I'm sure there are giant hairy spiders

and flappy bats with shifty eyes, lurking in the dark!"

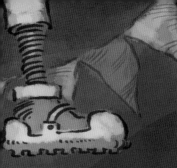
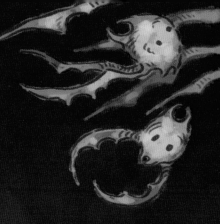

"Perhaps," said Big Brown. "But couldn't it also be
a smiley spacemen's zero-gravity birthday party?"

"Well, maybe," said Small Blue.

Big Brown turned on the light.

There were no spiders or bats.

There were no smiley spacemen, either.

Small Blue and Big Brown went into the kitchen.

"I bet there are warty witches and clackety skeletons,

sniff-sniff-sniffing, waiting for me in the dark," whispered Small Blue.

"There could be," said Big Brown.

"But I can imagine the kitchen playing host to a retired-pirates'

annual sock-knitting jamboree. Can't you?"

"I guess so," said Small Blue.

Big Brown turned on the light.

There were no witches or skeletons.

There were no retired pirates, either.

Small Blue helped Big Brown make two mugs of warm milk.

Then Small Blue looked out into the deep, dark night.

"What do you see?" Big Brown asked.

"Maybe the stars are running a relay race around the

moon while the planets cheer them on," she said.

"I think that's exactly right," said Big Brown.

They watched together until the last star

was safely over the finish line.

Small Blue yawned.

"Time to get back to bed," Big Brown said.

But Small Blue was already asleep.

Now if Small Blue wakes up in the deepest, darkest

hour of the night, she waves . . .

. . . just in case there are any
delightful doggies, smiley spacemen,
or retired pirates to wave back.